The Best Money Can Buy

By Matt Shea

"The Best Money Can Buy," by Matt Shea. ISBN 978-1-949756-56-2 (softcover); 978-1-949756-57-9 (eBook).

Published 2019 by Virtualbookworm.com Publishing Inc., P.O. Box 9949, College Station, TX 77842, US. ©2019, Matt Shea.

This Book Is Dedicated To My Daughter, Laura Marie Shea

My daughter, Laura, (pictured here with yours truly) has always made me happy. A happiness accompanied with many laughing sessions and a magic that keeps us both young forever. Laura, you are that one special girl whose always *my little girl.*

Hope you like the book!

Love you!

Dad

We Can't Forget the Cover

Thank you, Renèe, for finding time to add your artistic touch to another book cover for me- this being the fourth one!

It's only been the last three plus years Renèe considers living her second childhood through her artwork. She uses mainly acrylic paints but is adding watercolor and color pencil.

Also any photography in my books have been done by Renèe as well. She is currently collecting a series of photographs for an exhibition.

Renèe most enjoys the freedom in Expressive Abstracts, Representation, Impressionism and mixed media. She displays in local art shows, including the Seattle Recycle Art Fair. In just a few years, she has already been awarded Artist of the Month several times in the local art club. Additionally, she is a floral designer of 35 years, and continues to use her talents for weddings, home, office and church decor.

Renèe plans to have her own website in the near future,(she says," I'm a right brain person, techie stuff is Greek to me!") but for now you may contact her and view much of her artwork on Facebook at Artistic Xpressions by Renèe Klause.

Thanks again, Renèe. Looking forward to our next book cover!

Wishing you blessings.

Matt

A Special Thanks To
'This Week In America With Ric Bratton'

Matt Shea Books is grateful to Ric, his famous radio show; as well as his family and staff. Ever since my first paperback came out, *The Groundskeeper And Other Short Stories,* Ric has taken notice and extended his hand.

Ric has then gone further by encouraging me as a writer and being a friend throughout the year including birthdays and holidays. He has even sent me gift cards to coffee shops as a treat for the seniors I volunteer for!

All this from a radio personality heard the world over! A guy from the Eastern part of the country who took notice of my little operation on the West Coast.

Ric, thank you so much for entering our lives and always let me know if there is anything we can do for you!

And we love your show!

Matt and the gang

It's The 'Jupiter Rising Show'
Starring
Eileen Grimes
With Her Co-host Doug Johnston!

'The Jupiter Rising Show' is clearly one of the most talked-about radio shows from our area. It airs on 1150 AM on KKNW. This plays on Saturdays from 11:00 am to 12:00 noon and is located in Bellevue, Washington. It's a spontaneous talk show which evolves around world-renown astrologers Eileen Grimes and her co-host Doug Johnston. A potent combination where each exceeds twenty-eight years in the field!

After that, things begin to get a bit crazy...

Their guests range from fellow astrologers who are widely known, to other such personalities including famous psychics, authors(*like me)* and a host of various other interests that goes all directions. They even have a nut from Ireland who gets on once in a while. An amazing individual who has charmed the world with his fascination of tracking airline flights!

Eileen and Doug are also known to make an appearance at fairs and clubs. Eileen also has a very popular 'Readings After Dark'. A two-hour session at the famous Bur's Restaurant in Lakewood, Washington on Wednesday Nights. You can actually go back in time to a local landmark of seventy years, have a traditional home-cooked meal, meet Eileen and have her personally do a reading for you. It's from 6:30 pm to 8:30ish. It's an evening that will bring you back!

I guarantee !

I Can't express how fun it is when they allow me to join them on live radio! My friends and family all listen in, and rib me about it later...

Eileen and Doug; thanks for everything and let's go out to dinner soon!

And your show is fantastic!

Matt

Special Thanks

This writer has never covered any ground on his own. If I didn't have the Ella Rays and the Sally Jones out there who took the time to review my rough drafts and offer suggestions; I'd go nowhere.

Sally Jones out of Indiana was an educator for the elementary school system for thirty-nine years. She has also acted as a principle. She was unbelievably outstanding when it came to editing, storyline and encouragement. Sally proved to be an ideal fit for this project. For that, I thank her!

Ella Ray has been with me from the very start. Every one of my publications has been assisted by Ella's genius and dedication.

Girls: You're the best!

Matt-

Contents

Introduction

SOMEWHERE IN THE OUTSKIRTS of small-town USA lies a small oval track.

It can be found at the end of a lonely road nestled amongst the tall trees. An otherwise undeveloped area where only one house stood. It's here where the local legend had made a name for himself: Stanley Victor Hampton, alias *Rusty Hampton.*

This homegrown sprint car champion was every schoolboy's idol. The guy who usually won, visited classrooms and signed autographs. That *big brother* image who often remembered your name in the grocery store and wished you a good day.

When racing season was underway, this site was the most popular place in town. On more than one occasion, famous names were even seen mingling in the pits!

On any given day, somewhere, someone in town was mentioning the thirty-two year old's name. It seemed that the wiry, handsome man who stood at 6'-1" with dark brown hair and Frank Sinatra-blue eyes had it all: a fast racer, a beautiful wife, and the charisma that would surely cast him a leading role in Hollywood.

There was another side to the coin, however.

Much like the many who wanted to grow up to be just like him, he, too, had a quest that eluded him throughout life. *A feeling that something was always missing.*

The dashing man who always had a float in the local parades and fans who emulated him on Halloween *always felt an emptiness deep inside*. Throughout life, this product of adoption yearned to know *who* he actually was. More important, he needed to find out *why he was different...*

And now our story begins.

Chapter 1

SWEAT CONTINUED TO DRIP OFF Rusty Hampton's eyebrow as he polished the last wheel.

Upon finishing, he stood to use his tattered sleeve for a final time, wiping his face as if it were a washcloth. He stepped back and tossed a damp rag on his workbench. It was now time to inspect the labor of love just completed. Leaning forward, he meticulously began to survey the ever-important project that consumed his entire morning. Slowly, a concerned look became one of pride. Soon he could only marvel at what he was looking at.

What stood before him was a glistening display of four-wheeled modern art that turned heads. The latest in a long line of chariots that embraced his name in vibrant colors. A sparkling sensation that suggested he was getting closer to his childhood dream: *the Indy 500.*

Testimony that *races are won in the wintertime.*

It was moments like this that allowed the boy in one Rusty Hampton to come out. Doing a silent *Jitterbug step,* he walked out of his shop and entered an adjoining room.

Rusty was now in the other part of his *man cave,* where an old wooden desk and oversized leather chair awaited him. This grossly mismatched set fit in perfectly with the confines that smelled of Armor All and Windex. Rusty was in his element and leaned back, resting his feet on the desk.

Scanning from side to side, he glanced at the many framed newspaper articles that had his name in bold print.

Pictures that graced every local newsstand. All newcomers had their jaws drop when they saw that *two* display cases were needed to hold the many trophies he had won!

Souvenirs such as checkered flags, various car parts that had stories attached to them, and more framed pictures with celebrities were displayed in an unorthodox fashion. There was also an old coffee table that held racing programs from every event he ever entered. An old television set and a semi-obsolete computer helped balance out the equation.

There was more.

To the far left was the bathroom. A home-built do-it-yourself project that was still in progress — but functional! Finally, there was the customary 1970s off-white refrigerator that almost touched the backside of his desk (giving easy access).

What more could a man want?

All seemed in order as Stanley Victor Hampton reached over and placed a faded red baseball cap on his head. A trademark that had always followed him.

Questions now arise:

Why the hat; and where did the name 'Rusty' come from anyway?

To answer these questions, one would have to hold on to Rusty's hand and travel back twenty-five years. We now find our star sitting in front of a cake with seven lit candles...

⁊ↄ⸰ↄⷧ⸰ↄⷧↄⷧↄⷧ⸰ↄↄⷧↄ⸰

Stanley's seventh birthday found him surrounded by state workers who wore party hats. The employees put forth their best effort by wearing a smile while singing "Happy Birthday." When their shift ended, they wished him well and went home to their families.

The seven-year-old was once again left behind; but this time like a prisoner after visitation hours. The youth, who was recovering from two failed foster homes, was on a downward spiral in life. He now resided in a youth center that had him on probation.

It was obvious that Stanley was just another abandoned child who entered life like a hot potato — bouncing from one group care setting to another. At an early age he concluded one thing: that no one would ever have him *unless there was a payoff.*

It wasn't long after his birthday when a meaningful event changed his life.

He was on a mountain retreat with other boys his age. The counselors involved were a group of good men he had never met before. It was essentially a clean slate where no one seemed to know anyone's background- — or even care.

On this outing, he was treated like a man. When volunteers were asked to scout around for firewood, Stanley's hand immediately rose. Without receiving any cautions about the wilderness, he and others simply *went* to challenge the task. When it was time to fish, one of the men pointed at the gear and said, "You know what to do..."

It was the first day in his life where he felt *normal* and not branded by the stigma he had to start life with.

The outing then reached its pinnacle.

Rain drops started to lightly fall around the campfire. Drops that could only give a light sprinkle, but still required covering.

Stanley was enjoying every aspect of this trip and welcomed the rain. When asked if he would like to take shelter under a branch, he gave this response: "It's just a little rain. Besides, I like it!"

Then came a life-changing moment. A likeable old cuss said, "Then you better have this..." A red baseball cap appeared from nowhere and was placed on his head.

Stanley peered under the visor and replied, "Gee, thanks!"

"Why don't you keep it?" suggested the old man. "Then we can call you *Rusty*..."

The boy was flabbergasted to be gifted a grownup hat and questioned his good luck. "Really?" he replied.

"Really!" explained the man as he reached over to shake *Rusty's* hand.

Wonderful emotions hit the boy on all sides. Among other things, he liked the sound of 'Rusty.' Knowing that it would be the furthest thing from an insult, he wanted to know more. "Why Rusty?" he asked.

"Its a perfect name for an honorable rugged guy like you — even if you don't have red hair," said the old timer. "Don't worry," he chuckled. "With this hat and that great character of yours, you'll make a fine Rusty!"

The other counselors all put in their two cents' worth.

"That name is perfect for you!"

"You are a 'Rusty' if I ever saw one!"

"You will get famous with that name!"

"The girls are going to tear you apart!"

Rusty beamed with pride accepting his new name. For the rest of that trip he wore his hat and was known as 'Rusty.' *A name he loved!*

The night at the campfire changed his life. The boy who was still searching for a family had just acquired his first milestone:

He established his identity.

Chapter II

THE UPCOMING WEEKEND was especially important for Rusty Hampton. It was Golden Hills' annual Spring Spectacular.

A two-day event where the main drag of town was closed off for the celebration. This stretch of three blocks would have exhibits and displays from local businesses and charities, along with the school system making its presence known. Vendors along with clowns, jugglers, and musicians would fill in the gaps.

It was here where our champion always stole the show. The latest # 37 would once again be the main draw where flocks would gather to meet Rusty. The white man-eater with rich gold, red, and black highlights was further enhanced by the dazzling trophies that surrounded it, all dancing in unison under the sun. It was as if a rock concert was about to start.

Despite the many artifacts that spelled out glory, there was one more touch that surpassed everything: The slender, attractive woman who handed out autographed pictures and helped sell shirts. His one-of-a-kind wife, Jean. The model wore one of the lively *'Go! Rusty, Go!'* shirts that had a picture of his car, along with his number and a checkered flag.

❧❧❧❧❧❧❧

Jean Marie Hampton was the Florence Nightingale in Rusty's life.

The 5'–2" beauty with long blonde hair and blue eyes was of a quiet, sophisticated nature. She also held a record in Rusty's life: Jean was the sole survivor from his early childhood, being the only one having known him since grade school. *It was as if she was the soul mate he needed in life.*

True, opposites have been know to attract, but this phenomena seemed to go off into infinity. Rusty's marriage was indeed one of unconditional love, not one where each complimented the other.

It would be safe to say that Jean was watching over the boy she secretively cheered for. *The one who was dealt an unfair hand from the very beginning.*

Chapter III

JEAN MADE A MODEST INCOME as a school teacher. It was her frugal, sensible ways, however, that allowed the married couple with no children to survive. This was necessary because her better half had a taxing career that drained them on a regular basis. Despite Jean's stringent guidelines, Rusty's racing always took them back a step.

The objective behind any racer is to have their passion support itself *and hopefully leave something for their back pockets.* Long ago, if a driver won, he brought home a paycheck that more than covered all the expenses. Those days, however, had ended long ago because of the ever-increasing costs to get a competitive entry on the circuit. This was why such non-racing events as the Spring Spectacular were so important for Team Hampton. It was their opportunity to drum up sponsors, revenue that greatly surpassed any first-place prize money.

Rusty always made the first move when bills had to be addressed, a noble concept that did come with a drawback. He was much like the amateur golfer who refused to work anywhere except at a golf course when not in a tournament.

Rusty would focus on his 'home away from home' and confront track owner Rodney Phillips. "Rod, those bleachers are in need of some repair. How about I take care of it this week, and then touch up the grounds?"

Rodney's response would be a silent look of respect from his sincere brown eyes. Next he would place a hand on Rusty's shoulder. That was his way of saying *I like that idea.*

Rusty needed Rod, and Rod needed Rusty. If the sixty-two-year-old man with gray hair and a hunched figure didn't have a military pension along with a few rental homes, the track would have been abandoned years ago.

Rusty was more than his main draw; he was the best hired hand he ever had. He would work at any level and outperform other contractors without any complaints. All the extras came when Rusty was on the job. Once finished, he accepted whatever the track owner could afford and was grateful for it.

From there he proudly reported to the *boss* and gave Jean all the money. The Power of Attorney would then count it and give him an allowance. These transactions were always finalized by receiving a kiss on the cheek.

Rusty's efforts were of some help, but only closed the gap a bit...

❦❦❦

A racing team striving to be on top needs financial backing. Unless one is independently wealthy or has an inordinate amount of sponsors and volunteers, the conquest is impossible.

That is, unless you have *dear old Dad* coming to the rescue.

Chapter IV

IT WOULD BE AN UNDERSTATEMENT to say that Rusty Hampton was *once bitten, twice shy* when it came to outside help. His miserable track record with foster homes and various state facilities had given him great cause.

When Paul Hampton and his wife, Dottie, went through the adoption process like gangbusters to select him, the boy could only question. He wondered if it was just another attempt for the system to make him feel wanted as everyone went through the motions.

The initial phase of this acculturation was an awkward emotional swing for the bewildered eight-year-old. He was once again being encouraged to play *make-believe* that this set of strangers were now his parents. There was also something else thrown into the mix that was foreign to him.

The Hamptons were very wealthy and socialized with the upper crust. Dottie was stunningly beautiful with lively blonde hair. Her blue eyes were highlighted with lashes and liner that would rival Cleopatra.

Paul looked as wealthy as he was. His clean-shaven face, dignified brown eyes and perfectly groomed, thinning hair always commanded respect.

In time, Rusty knew that there was never any doubt that they wanted him as their own. But *why?*

Months after the legal transaction took place, the boy started to feel at home and more readily accepted hugs. In time, the titles of *mom and dad* were addressed with more sincerity.

There was one thing that he always remembered. His new family liked the name *Rusty* and thought he looked cute in his hat. Life was now different having a stable family. There were nights spent in front of the fireplace with a cup of hot cocoa, and others when his parents took him and a friend out for pizza. Birthday parties came with a bang, and the holidays matched the ones on television commercials.

Still, Rusty was a young boy with a mind that could deceive him if left alone too long. It happened one night, when he felt that it was time to *run away from home*. This was based on various reasons that he conjured up. Scenarios that didn't even remotely apply to his pampered situation with a dash of peer pressure thrown in.

The fleeing young man only had phase one of his exit planned out. He would walk a few blocks to a trail that led through a park. At the end of that trail was a small wooden structure that resembled a church from a past century. Inside the tiny, one-room sanctuary with stained glass were two pews that faced an altar. It was there the boy wearing the red baseball cap spent a cold night staring at a miniature-sized replica of Jesus. The next morning he awoke at dawn, only to be surprised. Someone had placed a Bible in his arms and an army blanket over his body.

Realizing that he had nowhere to go, the hungry, frightened boy ran home and returned to his bedroom undetected; or so he thought. He would keep his Bible for the rest of his life, glancing at it periodically when time allowed. Hiding it under his pillow until he became an adult.

Nothing was ever mentioned about his first and only attempt to run away.

Not long after that escapade, his prominent father decided to flex his muscle. He would simply 'buy the boy' and surprised him with a gift that no ten-year-old would ever turn down. There, waiting in the garage, was a gasoline-powered go-kart with a helmet resting in the seat. "Well, what do you think, son?" asked the stepfather in a smug tone.

The kid fell into rank without any thought. Looking up at the middle-aged man, he said, "Wow! I love it, Dad; and I love you!" Rusty then hugged the man who'd made him happy.

Immediately the boy ran to the cart, put the helmet on, sat in the seat and grabbed the wheel. "Wow!" he said. "This is so neat!"

"Do you have a number picked out for your racer?" asked the stepdad.

Without any thought, the boy had an immediate response: "Number 37!"

Paul was intrigued that his son already knew what number he wanted to race under. "Why that number?" he asked.

"Part of it's from the Bible. Number three represents the trinity of the Father, Son and Holy Spirit. And seven is known for being *lucky seven*. I'll use both of them in that order to let God know that I'm racing with him, and that I might need some luck..."

Paul was greatly impressed with his son's advanced answer and could only marvel at him.

From there, the boy got out of the cart and addressed his *dad* with requests. "Can I get a wing on it and get it painted, like the Indy 500 guys do?"

"Why, sure you can," replied the rich man. "You can have whatever you see fit for your racer." It was at that moment when Paul Hampton said something that would always define what he was in life:

"It will be the best money can buy."

More hugs of gratitude followed with Paul Hampton having won his battle. The father-son team were now well bonded, with the motorized toy being their common ground.

In months to follow, if his homework was done, he could go riding. Locally there were defunct businesses that offered huge abandoned parking lots *just waiting for them*. Many afternoons were spent watching the boy who'd just turned eleven whiz by as he slid into a turn.

"Don't you think that this is too dangerous?" a concerned Dottie Hampton would ask.

"It's just a phase," said her husband as he put his arm around her. "A few years from now, he'll be in medical school..."

Paul Hampton couldn't have been more wrong. What he had actually done was *create a monster*.

When Rusty learned of a nearby track that taught racing fundamentals, his dad opened up his wallet. Soon the banker ponied up for an advanced 'state-of-the-art' racer with all the extras, including a personalized paint job with matching attire. His *future doctor* was now officially competing in what would be considered *the little league of racing*.

Glory would soon follow, throwing more kindling on the fire. In time, an occasional picture in the paper and another third-place trophy would be enshrined in Rusty's room. All of this, while his parents sat in the stands shaking in fear, holding hands while flinching at every turn *and praying*.

This cruel form of drama reached its peak one Saturday. There was a pile-up on the track, which resulted in carts flying and one driver being thrown from his machine. A small fire ensued with track marshals running to the scene. In moments, Car #37's driver was taken away in an ambulance. The parents who watched had their hearts skip a beat. In fact, a terrified Dottie almost fainted.

The following day had the local newspaper capture the entire event. In bold print, the headlines read:

HAMPTON SURVIVES FIERY WRECK!

On the front page was a series of pictures showing the wreck. It also showed Rusty in a hospital bed with a broken arm while giving a thumbs-up. *The boy was now the most popular figure in town, with cards and flowers being sent from near and far.* Later, he was interviewed by the press as well as the local television stations.

Rusty relished the attention. Wearing the streamlined dark sunglasses that the big boys wore, he answered questions and signed autographs. Then he made an announcement. "I'll be back in an even better cart, *and it will be the best money can buy...*"

In time, Rusty's dad was the 'go-to guy' when money became an issue. *Pop* rarely failed.

As Rusty Hampton grew, tension occasionally mounted between him and the high society couple who'd adopted him. True, they did pick him out of many and never failed him. Still, his nature marched to a different beat.

Through time, he had two names when it came to referring to his parents. There was the traditional 'mom and dad'.

Then the other name, that could only be mentioned out of hearing range.

When the waters got rough, he could only think of the many pictures they had of themselves throughout their lavish home. Ones that had the Great Pyramids of Egypt in the background, or other elite landmarks known throughout history.

His stepdad's firmness when using money as leverage and his stepmother's well-spoken etiquette and matching jewelry always rubbed him wrong. In fact, it reminded him of a specific couple who'd graced *television-land* years ago. Ones who were filthy rich and marooned on a desert island with peasants.

For those of you who guessed The Howells, you're right!

Chapter V

RUSTY HAD BIG THINGS GOING on with his racing future. There was the town fair coming up with the first race of the season the following week. All looked good with #37 well-machined, washed and polished.

His gun for success was fully loaded. *He just needed the financial backing to put it all in motion...*

It was now time to *fact and figure* how much there actually was to support this endeavor. When the grand total fell relatively short, *plan B* was put into action. *The process of elimination.*

Mentally, Rusty mulled over the few friends he felt comfortable confiding in. One by one, each had an excuse as to why they weren't in a position to see their friend through. Like any man, there was nothing he hated more than being painted into a corner.

It was time to visit the Howells.

⌇⤫⊘⌇⤫⊘⌇⤫⊘

Dinner with his parents was a surprisingly warm affair that went Rusty's way. It all started with his stepmom running out to the car as he and Jean pulled up. When he stepped out, she hugged him while placing a check in his pen pocket.

An apparent peace offering from the powwow they had at their last meeting.

Days before, Paul Hampton had struck a nerve with his adopted son by offering him a position that most would kill for. *A seat with the big boys—if he played the game right.*

The racecar driver with his own identity had a knee-jerk response. He simply put on his red hat and walked out the front door.

As usual, dinner was catered by one of the county's most elite restaurants. In moments, gourmet food and rich ice cream desserts were delivered by a man in a three-piece suit.

The evening was one of warmth and appreciation. The parents were now on good behavior and only looked at the positive aspects of their boy's life. He *was* a well-respected, honorable person who could not have married any better. *Paul and Dottie absolutely loved Jean.*

The after-dinner fireside ritual went well. It ended on the right note, allowing a relationship with Rusty to continue. A calm setting where stories were exchanged with immense laughter.

When it was time to call it an evening, a final round of hugs and appreciation were traded one last time.

"Remember, Rusty," said his dad, fighting back tears. "This is *your* home too. You are always welcome here; let us know if there is anything we can *ever* do for you and Jean." Paul's firm handshake became a warm hug.

"Thanks, Dad," replied Rusty. "You and Mom have always been the best thing that has ever happened to us."

He was right.

On the drive home, Jean asked her husband a question. "Well, how was your evening?"

After a lengthy pause he took a deep breath and replied, "Mom and Dad were great, as usual."

Jean agreed and gave her man a peck on the cheek.

❧❧❧

The following day had Rusty Hampton twenty-five thousand dollars richer. Without hesitation he went to the bank, and then visited the few he owed money to. Once his debts were settled, he contacted his three-man pit crew.

"Dinner is on us tonight. The plan is that we'll meet at Bev's Steakhouse at seven—and bring your dates!"

That night, Rusty Hampton and his racing team were the talk of the town. Many reported seeing them at the renowned hot spot, with a few autographs being signed.

The entire party included:

(1) Rusty.
(2) His wife, who was 'the mom' of the operation and the vendor who wore the popular racing shirt seen throughout town. Jean also made sandwiches for the hungry crew and filled in the gaps on race day.
(3-4) Cliff Wright, his crew chief and main mechanic. A former racer himself who was involved with every charitable program that the town had to offer. A heavyset figure pushing two hundred and fifty pounds, he was as gentle as a lamb. His retro crew cut, smile, and penetrating blue eyes immediately set anyone he met at ease. Cliff's wife, Sandra, sat next to him. A nice, quiet, librarian type with the wire-rimmed glasses and bun hairstyle to prove it.
(5-6-7-8) Roger Blackstone and his brother, Ed. The Blackstone brothers were classmates with Rusty from the day he entered town. The identical twins with bald heads and goatees were a *hoot*. Their lanky appearances, along with the wild brown eyes and the antics they were known for, amused those who knew them *or even saw them*. When it came time to work as a team, they were the best in the business.

It was a given that the brothers would arrive with girlfriends. Candace was Roger's girl. The short brunette with chestnut eyes was a pistol! At camp outs she was known to whistle a country mile and play the harmonica.

Mary belonged to Ed and was of a more quiet nature. The redheaded beauty with blue eyes and average height always downplayed the many beauty pageants she competed in. Mary also possessed an incredible wit about herself that left many in stitches.

They were all there; one big, happy family. All at once, Rusty passed out envelopes to Cliff, Roger and Ed. "Go ahead," cried out Rusty. "Open it up!" What each found was a thousand dollars for their keeping. Eyes looked dumbfounded at one another as jaws dropped in astonishment.

Rusty continued, "What you guys do for me as volunteers, and the many times you picked up the tab, I think you deserve at least this much."

A humble *thank you* was returned as their dates smiled in approval. Rusty then received an ovation, which included a kiss from his wife. Eventually, he excused himself to visit the restroom with Jean following suit. Before he entered the bathroom, his wife gave him another passionate kiss on the lips—and removed his wallet from his pocket at the same time. Cleverly, she walked backwards into the lady's restroom with wallet in hand and a sarcastic smile on her face.

She returned in a moment, handing him a fraction of what he had. "This should be enough to pay for the dinner, and the rest is your allowance for the next two weeks." From there she handed him his thin billfold and returned to the feast.

Gazing at the woman he loved, Rusty recalled the times when they were clearly poverty-stricken. Times when they were forced to live out of his truck because of his on-again, off-again irresponsible lifestyle. Moments that seemed so hopeless that the couple had to resort to secluded hostels on the outskirts of no-name towns. Places that served as a safety net for stranded travelers and the losers of society.

One episode played back in his mind when entering such a hellhole. "Hey! *Aren't you Rusty Hampton*?" called out a down-and-out residence. "Wow!" exclaimed the middle-aged man in need of a bath and clean clothing. "I bet you're here to talk to us about drugs and alcohol." The vagabond's sighting caused a small commotion as fellow derelicts came out of nowhere to see the famed driver they'd always heard of.

Jean gave a sharp elbow to his ribs, saying:

Matt Shea

"You'll fit in here just perfectly, and all you have to do is not change a bit..."

Chapter VI

RACE DAY FINALLY ARRIVED with Team Hampton in good spirits. As always, the grounds were packed for the first event of the year, with many having come to watch Rusty win!

The many hours of hard work and preparation were about to pay off for the reigning champion. Everything was checked and double-checked, from the proper fuel mixture to the pressure in each tire. Not only was his entry proven to be the fastest in qualifying; he was also a crowd favorite.

All seemed to be in order when Rusty Hampton decided to take a break. It was now time for him to go for a walk and clear his head.

At that moment, something peculiar seemed to internally call out to him. It was as if he was being summoned to walk a certain path, to arrive at a certain point—at the exact right time. An intervention of sorts.

If there was anyone who knew to listen their instincts, it was Stanley Victor 'Rusty' Hampton.

As the famous racer approached a concession stand, fate presented itself. What he saw was an innocent boy being tormented and bullied by others who were probably classmates. This cruel verbal assault that targeted an overweight body with a passive nature brought back memories. In the early years of Stanley's life, he too was a constant victim of rejection and isolation.

The chicken had come home to roost, and now it was Rusty's turn.

Without any thought, he kicked it into high gear and addressed the fourteen-year-old with straight brown hair. "Where have you been?" he exclaimed. Everything stopped as the group saw that it was none other than *Rusty Hampton himself* in his racing suit. Placing a hand on the boy's shoulder, he continued, "We got a race to win today, and we can't do it without you..."

The ruffians looked at one another in astonishment. Immediately they began to realize that they were picking on the wrong person. "C'mon," ordered Rusty. "We've got less that an hour." The boy with soulful brown eyes looked up, smiled at his hero, and left with him.

"What's your name?" asked Rusty as they walked away.

"David Smith," he replied.

Rusty formally introduced himself and followed with a handshake. Next he patted his new friend on the back, saying," Don't worry about those guys; you're with us now."

Rusty was brilliant when it came to non-verbal communication. As he entered his pit, it was understood within a minute that David would be with them for the day. All came forward with smiles and open hands. One by one he met Cliff, the Blackstone brothers, and Jean. He pointed at the display that sold the hats and shirts, with Jean knowing what to do. Handing David a size that would fit him, she said, "You're going to look great in this!" Soon the rescued boy was part of the team, with a uniform to prove it!

It was now time to put some icing on the cake. As David was putting on his new shirt and hat, Rusty conferred with his crew.

One of the greatest thrills racing has to offer is to stand next to a high-performance engine while it's warming up. The popular

#37 had its back axle elevated on jacks, *with one David Smith told to climb into the car!*

"Wow!" exclaimed the enthused youth. Once fastened in, Rusty spun the engine to life. In the seat sat a brave David Smith, holding onto the wheel with a crowd gathering around. David shook with the hundreds of horsepower that pounded the entire car. Rusty looked at Ed and pointed to a small canister that contained a rich solvent. Soon flames were coming out of the pipes as David held on. Rusty leaned over the engine and revved it a few times while checking for leaks.

Everything checked out as the driver smiled in approval. On that note, he manually shut off the engine from where he stood. Immediately, the crowd went nuts and gave an ovation, with a proud David Smith having the time of his life.

｡ぺ⊚⁄｡ぺ⊚⁄｡ぺ⊚⁄｡

It was a perfect outing for Team Hampton —the professional who worked at that very racetrack tested his mount and sharpened his skills at every opportunity. He was more than ready to win all the marbles that day!

The introduction of David was a good fit. He performed his assigned tasks well and got along with everybody. When the trophy was presented, Rusty made sure that David was front and center, *with his name spelled right.*

The long day ended with Rusty meeting David's mother, Gail Smith. "Thank you so much for what you did for my son!" said the woman in her fifties with curly gray hair and green eyes. Hugging Rusty, she continued in tears, "He's such a good boy, and everybody picks on him."

"You don't have to worry about that now," said Rusty in a reassuring voice as he patted her on the back. "He'll be with us for the rest of the season—and that's extended to you as well."

A conversation ensued where Rusty learned more about the fatherless boy. The woman explained how they lived with her sister and went to church often. "It's the one place where he'll always be accepted."

The following day had many newspapers covering the race. All had Rusty's name in bold print. They also showed pictures of the crew posing with the trophy. This included one David Smith front and center, *with his name spelled correctly.*

Chapter VII

LIFE WAS ALWAYS DIFFERENT when the racing season got underway. It was one of a systematic pattern, where the next race was always top priority and team meetings mandatory.

The result?

More first-place trophies, with additional sponsors wanting to get in on the act. Soon, local TV commercials followed, with the mighty #37 paying for itself *including dinner money, if nothing broke.*

The *Pride Of Golden Hills* image had skyrocketed, with extra grandstands having to be added. Every race day brought fans who would stand up and erratically wave their arms while yelling out his name. *Rusty loved it!* Some days he would see his parents in the stands wearing pullovers with his team logo. On others, it was *The Howells* in their tacky tropical vacation garb, with their stupid Hawaiian Punch hats.

Regardless, their boy *did* acknowledge them.

There was also an added dimension that put a different spin on the team's chemistry: David, *the son Rusty never had.*

Rusty's crusade for the fatherless boy mirrored his own past. For years he hungered for acceptance and unconditional love. *It was now time for him to answer the call and give back.*

This endeavor would be more than just a day of the boy's life with broken promises to follow. It was a commitment to always be there, *with a bond that implied family.* After all, Rusty and his wife had something in common with Paul and Dottie. *Each had no siblings, with the women not able to produce children of their own.*

The Howells fell in love at first sight when they met the timid boy. Soon, it was common practice to have David's small family join theirs when a special occasion presented itself. Holidays, birthdays, barbeques, and other such events were graced by the addition of David. Rusty would even visit his school with his immaculate racing machine and give talks about having a good direction in life. Later, he'd swing by unannounced to check up on David's grades and take the household out for ice cream.

In time it was apparent that his plight in life was actually filling a void in theirs. The popular addition to Team Hampton was now feeling that *he belonged.* Not only did a smidgen of small-town celebrity status rub off on him, but he was now *making friends in school.*

⁂

One day it happened: Rusty's *other side* was unleashed at the boy who was now fifteen.

It all took place in the pits after another consecutive win. The hoopla had died down, with the racing team gathering tools and pushing the car into its trailer. Like any Marlboro commercial, the victory was finished out with the winning driver enjoying a cigarette, a crude habit that even Rusty wasn't proud of. Often he'd go days without one, while only smoking half when he did. In one motion, Rusty dropped the lit cigarette and began to walk in the opposite direction.

Imitation is the highest form of flattery

As the cigarette fell to the ground, the adolescent scavenged it and placed the filter in his mouth. Rusty caught the event from the corner of his eye and spun back around with a look that equaled an irate drill sergeant.

Steel blue eyes outlined by a tightened face marched up to the petrified boy.

"*What are you doing?*" asked the mentor in a raised voice.

The teen shook like a leaf and stuttered at the first word. "I-I..."

It was never Rusty's intention to frighten his young crew member. In seconds he got a hold of himself and dropped his shoulders. "Look," he said in a fatherly voice. "Those things are bad for any of us." Without having an order barked at him, David took it out of his mouth and dropped it on the ground. Following the *Hippocratic Oath* to the letter, he then pointed at it and said, "They only belong in the garbage."

"Sorry, sir," came an obedient reply. Rusty looked upward, rolling his eyes, and then pulled out a pack of cigarettes. "We need each other!" he exclaimed. "How about you and me forming a pact on this very day, at this very moment? We can get these horrible things out of our lives, *now!*"

David knew right from wrong and smiled while nodding his head. "Do we have a deal?" asked Rusty with his hand extended.

"We got a deal!" responded David as the two buds shook hands.

"Good!" cried Rusty. "*Nobody in my life is going to miss this stuff.*" At once, the racing legend placed the pack into the same trash container that held the cigarette last touched by David.

Rusty would continue his life keeping his end of the agreement.

There were still more issues to address.

Rusty got closer and placed a warm hand on the boy's shoulder. Leaning toward him, he asked a question in a soft tone, "What made you do something like that, when you're so smart?"

Looking straight at the man he admired, David gave his answer. "I wanted to be a famous race car driver like you."

"What?" responded Rusty with a perplexed expression on his face. Standing up, he looked away to gather his thoughts. Once composed, he cleared his throat and faced the impressionable youth.

"Did it ever occur to you that I was trying to be more like you?" said the local star in the red hat. David tensed up, trying to fathom what just came out of his idol's mouth. Rusty continued.

"Look, this is something that you don't want to be doing," he said with direct eye contact. The boy stood still and gave his undivided attention. "It's a hard life that usually doesn't grant anything," he stressed. "For most, it's only for the thrill of the moment—and that's it! Trust me," said his mentor. "There's more to life than racing."

Looking up to the heavens, he stretched out his arms for assistance and abruptly said, "Wait here; I've got something for you." He left and returned in a few minutes.

"There is something magic about this book," said Rusty as he showed his prized Bible. "It entered my life when I was trying to choose a better path."

David's face glowed in approval. His small household frequented church often, with him being very aware of what the Good Book stood for. What amazed him was that he never knew his big brother and friend also had a relationship with it.

"It's full of good stuff that will guide you through your worst problems, *if you'll let it*," he assured David. "I read it as often as I can, *especially at night*. Every time I look through it, I get more out of it!"

Rusty got even closer and dropped to one knee. *"I like it even better than my red hat!"* he whispered.

David's grin was now ear-to-ear.

Rusty handed the Bible over to David, saying, "Here, I want you to have this."

David looked down at his spiritual gift and replied, "Gee, thanks!" The young man was now speechless and could only marvel. A moment of silence had passed when a worrisome expression covered the boy's face. In a trembling voice, he looked up to Rusty and asked a question. "Does this mean that I'm not on the team anymore?"

Rusty was two steps ahead and had an immediate answer.

"You have to stay here until I grow up, *and that's going to be a very long time from now!*"

A relieved boy stood before him as Jean's voice gave an additional comment. "I can only agree."

A peck on the cheek followed, giving assurance that Rusty Hampton was indeed on the right track.

Chapter VIII

TEAM HAMPTON CONTINUED ITS WINNING WAYS with a few more sponsors joining the bandwagon. This expansion also brought forth tantalizing offers.

Distant tracks offered him money to race there as a drawing card. Shopping malls and automotive outlets were crying out to have the classy driver and his magic #37 make an appearance. Radio personalities were also making contact along with noble charities experiencing the good side of Rusty Hampton when time allowed. Soon it was *Rusty* taking his parents out to the finest restaurants known in the county. Outings that hushed his worst critics. *"That's our boy!"* Paul would whisper into Dottie's ear.

When the long, arduous season finally came to an end, the team found itself at an awards banquet. The recognition they received for their stellar performance seemed endless. It was now time to harvest. Handshakes, plaques, trophies, pictures, praises, autographs, questions, a fat check, ovations, and more handshakes came from all directions.

As if that weren't enough, prominent racing magazines also expressed their interest in the dynamic *Rusty Hampton.*

Life was good!

❧ ✦❧❦✦❧ ✦❧✦

Months after their winning season had come to a close, a milestone in life had presented itself. *Their latest member was now eligible to get a driver's license.*

"Let *me* teach you how to drive," insisted Rusty.

One might ask: *Where does a famous dirt track racer teach a student to drive a vehicle?*

The answer? *On a dirt track, of course!*

Being the star and a hired hand at the local track gave Rusty unlimited access, with no permission required.

After school, Rusty took David to the track and gave him a heart-to-heart about driving. "Do you know why we're here?" he asked David.

There was a long pause, and then the teen took a guess. "To learn how to race like you do?"

"You'll never be racing anything," replied the instructor. "I want to introduce you to driving the hard way. If a guy can drive safely on loose dirt, he can drive safely anywhere."

David got a visual from the explanation given and digested the concept. Realizing that it would compare to keeping balanced while walking on ice, he looked at Rusty and nodded his head in understanding.

The rest of the daylight hours were spent with David using trial and error behind the wheel. Despite the many times he slid, spun, or kicked up an unnecessary amount of dirt, Rusty remained patient while giving tips and offering encouragement. "You're doing amazing so far!" he would call out. "Just remember to never be in a hurry, and to always be calm."

In essence, it was like a barber who must be able to shave a balloon without popping it.

The driving lesson carried on for weeks with David gaining confidence and showing steady improvement. The tame rhythm escalated to where the student eventually found himself with the *big boys*. He was now driving on side streets and mastering the art of parallel parking.

Time and time again, Rusty would sit down with David and talk about safe driving. He would especially reiterate over and over about overconfident, reckless drivers and the influence of alcohol. *"If you want to get ten steps ahead of your age group, never, ever touch the stuff—under any conditions!"* he advised.

David aced his written test and greatly impressed the state instructor with his cautious driving.

❦ ❦ ❦

Acquiring a driver's license in high school grants mega-kudos to anyone. Even the family Rambler gets into the act by becoming a *chick magnet* on a Saturday night. Despite one David Andrew Smith advancing to the majors, he was still cursed by his renowned clean lifestyle. A non-threatening image that just wasn't *cool enough,* despite his Hampton connection.

Three cheers for Rusty!

Still, regardless of who you are, there will always be that certain someone who loves you *just the way you are...*

The humble *Lisa Grimes* was such a person, a fellow semi-overweight student who had a crush on David since day one.

Q) Why David, you might ask?

A) Because like attracts like; that's why!

Lisa knew him as the boy she always saw in church. The 'man of the family' who always accompanied his mother and aunt. A self-sacrificing, non-judgmental soul with a pure heart. That passionate being who stood for justice and projected love through innocent eyes.

There was more: Each had brown hair with matching eyes and stood at almost the same height. If seen in public, they could easily be passed off as siblings, a comfort for the girl who was dealt the same hand. *She too had no brothers or sisters, and had never known her biological father.*

It was a given that Lisa could only love a boy who shared the same pain...

❦ ❦ ❦

One night at the local pizza parlor, Jean asked David if he was seeing anyone. He blushed between bites and said, "Nah."

Jean was more in-tune with his age group than given credit and probed deeper. "Well, being a woman, I know for a fact that there would be at least a few out there who would be interested in you..."

Rusty noticed David turning a mild shade of red. Next, he began to squirm in an attempt to change the subject. Winking at his wife, he looked back at David with a grin of curiosity. "C'mon, out with it!" he barked in a jovial tone.

"Welll..." he replied in a soft, high pitch.

David paused to gather his thoughts and began to talk about Lisa. He covered how he knew her and passed her off as a *friend*.

"That's what Jean and I are," said Rusty as his wife pecked his cheek.

"It all starts with friendship," Jean added. "It's the *friendship* that needs to stay alive for a relationship to make it."

David began to think.

Rusty leaned close and whispered out loud, *"What does she look like?"*

David's initial description was less than flattering. He demonstrated his age by focusing on her weight and plain looks.

Rusty spread his arms and cried out, *"What's wrong with that?"*

"David," injected Jean. "It's all about being credited for what you are as a person—without any deception getting in the way."

The woman of wisdom then delivered the knockout punch. "She seems to be just as wonderful as you are. Why, she'd fit in here perfectly."

Those words took him back to the day when none other than Rusty Hampton himself chose him. *Changing his life forever.*

A week later, Rusty was walking hand in hand with Jean. All at once she nudged him and pointed across the street. What they saw was David leaving the local hamburger stand in his mom's outdated Buick. Sitting next to him was a girl who could have passed for his sister *or wife*. The teens were too happy to notice, or even care that they were detected. They simply drove off with an evening ahead of them.

A tear ran down Rusty's face as he spoke under his breath. *"That boy's going to make it."*

Chapter IX

THE RACING WORLD is much like the game of billiards: *Each shot must set you up for the next*. Team Hampton's winning ways had dwindled the local competition to a distant second. This in turn drew attention to the bigger and better, more elite camps. To the racing world, it was quite clear that this driver was overdue to step up to the higher ranks. *Much higher...*

One day it happened *like in the movies...*

The most important phone call of his entire career had arrived, with legendary motor sports mogul Rocco Valentine Conti on the other end.

The renowned tycoon who always hired the best drivers knew a surprising amount about the racer from Golden Hills. Using his beautiful Italian-American voice, he greeted with charm.

"Hello my friend! This is Rocco Valentine Conti; I'd like to speak to Rusty Hampton."

The distinct accent and directness left no doubt that he was indeed talking to the man who always fielded champions. "Well, how are you today, Mr. Conti? This is Rusty!"

"Please, call me Rocco," came a warm response.

A conversation ensued where compliments joined with laughter were exchanged. In time, Rocco got to the nitty-gritty and discussed why he was calling. "I think you'd do well in the Indy 500," he said.

Rocco's comment brought new life to Rusty's childhood heroes. Visions of Mario Andretti, A. J. Foyt and Vukovitchs danced in his head. Pancho Carter and a host of others followed. Men who gambled their lives on small tracks across the country while challenged to put food on the table. A rare breed that would one day find their place in history, ever since the wheel was invented. Rusty was holding his breath in hopes that his contact would go in that direction. "That has been my goal since childhood!" he replied.

"You wouldn't be a racer if it wasn't," came the response.

The meeting was brief and broke the ice. From there, Rocco extended himself and offered to take his entire family and pit crew out to dinner. "That would be great!" came an enthusiastic reply. Arrangements would be made by Rocco to meet at the best restaurant in Golden Hills the following month. All would be there.

There was also a catch. The tycoon finished the call by informing Rusty that he was making arrangements to assemble a fundraiser via sprint cars. Rusty knew exactly why such an impromptu event came up on such short notice. It was an obvious last- minute precautionary measure that would allow him to get a closer look at *his man in action*. "It will be great to sit with your parents and watch you race," said Rocco. "I'll also be with some associates who are dying to meet you."

Rusty knew the in and outs of racing—on and off the track. Knowing the score, he made a vow to himself:

If it's a movie star they want; it's a movie star they're going to get...

⸙⸙⸙

After the call, Rusty looked up to the sky and raised his arms. "You haven't let me down yet!" he cried out. Next, he made a beeline to his parents and told them the news.

"The Indy 500?" his dad repeated while holding onto his son's shoulders. *"The Indy 500?"*

"Our son is going to compete in the most famous race known to mankind—*and win it!*" cried out his mother as she hugged her boy.

⁀ᕱᕦᕱᕮ ᕱᕦᕱᕮ ᕱᕦᕱᕮ

In another corner of town, life was also taking shape for team member David Smith. The Bible his mentor had gifted him had taken control of the young man's life. Not only did he discover scriptures that were highlighted by a young Rusty Hampton years ago; he digested others. This intervention created a cute game of *tag, you're it*. Often, a favorite verse would be texted, only to have one of equal value volleyed back.

Such random messages would arrive at any time of day or night, and always received an immediate response that further glorified their faith. Also, *it wasn't always David who reached out first*.

The like-minded duo who definitely shared the ultimate bond found themselves at a crossroad that led to different worlds. One was daring to address the highest level known in racing, while the other was setting his sights to the fullest.

David wanted to serve our Lord.

Chapter X

RUSTY HAMPTON SUMMONED HIS PIT CREW for what he described to be *a very important team meeting.* It was agreed that they would meet at a local restaurant for breakfast in a reserved section. All were in awe when told of the good news. High-fives were exchanged at the table, with a feeling of accomplishment setting the mood.

The leader of Hampton Racing continued with an iron fist and got to specifics. The upcoming charity race and banquet was discussed next. "This is to test us!" Rusty emphasized. *"They can back out at anytime."*

Each member looked at one another with an understanding and remained quiet.

"We need to present ourselves as more than the crack professional team they know us to be. We have to *wow them* and exceed their wildest expectations. We have to look and perform as if we're training for the Olympics!" he said.

Rusty was already told where the benefit race would be held. It was across the state at a track that was considerably bigger than what he was accustomed to. True, he had raced there before—but he'd only placed well. This was because of the track's long straightaways that required more horsepower. Rusty's game was usually the dicing of smaller tracks and sliding into turns. A continuous battle on loose dirt, where the mastering of acceleration and counter-steering separated the men from the boys.

Engine wizard Cliff Wright knew exactly what to do. With ease, he would modify the engine for higher speeds. Ed and Roger would in turn set up Rusty's entry to fly past the competition once out of a turn.

The seasoned pro would take his mount to unpaved back roads and familiarize himself with faster speeds. Next he would rent the very racetrack he was to appear at and have intense practice sessions.

The mighty #37, along with its famed driver and polished crew, would be ready for their audition.

❧ ❦ ❧ ❦ ❧ ❦

Paul Hampton was also busy at work. He knew the world of money and did some research on one Rocco Valentine Conti. To his amazement, there was page after page about the man on the internet. Initially, facts about where he was born and his accolades in racing were brought to light. Names and places that didn't mean anything to the former broker. Soon he came across the many businesses he owned and associates he dealt with. Paul Hampton then became astonished, to say the least. *These were his heroes in the business world!* Leaning back, he gazed upward in wonderment.

His next visit with Rusty started off with a firm handshake full of large bills. "I'm so proud of you, son!" he said with direct eye contact. "You are now with my idols *because you're in their league.* You must accept this," said the voice of experience. "It's of the utmost importance that you keep up with them..."

Chapter XI

THE DAY ARRIVED WHEN RUSTY'S LIFE met with Rocco Conti and his wife, Maria.

The classy mogul from Italy insisted that his staff be allowed to make arrangements. What took place was the old adage that: *you can only make a first impression once.* The finest banquet room available was rented out, with all the trimmings thrown in. Red roses with victory balloons and checkered flags graced the lavish room fitted with brass, velvet, and chandeliers.

Directly front and center for all to see was an ice sculpture of the mighty number '37' along with another checkered flag.

Most important was Rocco himself, standing with his wife at the main entrance. The gracious man in the expensive three-piece suit stood dignified. Smiling, his hand was extended as an elated Rusty Hampton trotted up to him with open arms.

Everything started off on the right foot with introductions being made, followed by warm handshakes and sincere hugs. Soon, Rusty along with his entire family, crew, and their significant others were well-acquainted with Rocco and Maria. It was David and his girlfriend, however, who made the greatest impression on the regal couple from Italy.

Their topic?

The Christian faith and the many universal quotes from the Bible that were shared worldwide.

The celebration feast followed, with Rocco and his wife showing etiquette by sitting next to Rusty's parents. It was the highest honor one Paul Hampton ever felt in his entire life: *He* was having a dinner conversation with none other than Rocco Conti himself.

Their next visit would be sitting in the stands together, watching Paul's boy drive the race of his life...

❧❧❧

Race day arrived with Team Hampton's entry being pushed onto the track. Their mere presence immediately drew cheers from the packed house. Rocco, Maria, Paul, and Dottie were caught up in the moment and stood to join the ovation.

Throughout the day, it was Rusty's race. Despite the many entries, there was little competition for the seasoned champion. Rusty never lost sight that he was being evaluated by Rocco Conti to see how he would fare driving longer straightaways. Always one step ahead, his focus was one of fast speeds while maintaining control entering and exiting the turns—all with a smoothness that required little lane change. *The way an Indy 500 driver must perform.*

Rocco spent the outing peering through binoculars as he meticulously evaluated his prospect with a fine-toothed comb. On occasion, he'd release a sigh of approval while nodding his head. Paul knew to remain quiet as he beamed with pride.

Between rounds, a brief exchange of chit-chat circulated between the two couples. During the heats that led up to the final, Rocco was all business and gave his undivided attention to his man.

It was to be another win for Rusty Hampton. After the trophy presentation, Rocco motioned for Paul to follow him. Immediately, he led him to the dirt his son had just raced on and inspected his tracks. Rocco pointed out in astonishment on how they didn't show signs of *ever* having lost control. Looking at the proud father, he said with excitement:

"Wait until he gets on asphalt!"

That evening, Paul and Dottie had 'Team Hampton' over for some pie and coffee. An evening designed to toast one another for their recent success with Rocco Conti and the good things to follow.

The local news was turned on to watch the coverage of that day's race. To everyone's surprise, Rocco himself was interviewed, saying: "I need a third driver for next year's Indy 500, and found that Rusty Hampton is a good candidate..." Upon hearing what was said, the living room froze in silence with all eyes gazing at the once-fatherless boy...

Chapter XII

ONCE ROCCO CONTI PUBLICLY REVEALED that he was considering having Rusty Hampton drive for him, the media wasted no time.

The following morning headlines read:

'Hampton To Bid For Indy 500'

Reporters from radio and television made their move, as did a few auto magazines in quest of the latest craze. Always the professional, Rusty was his smooth, polished, happy-go-lucky self who credited his success to the town he lived in.

Life was good for the *#37* racing team. Children of all ages were knocking on his door and asking for autographs. Teens and housewives would request and receive selfies with him. The local hamburger stand even had *The Rusty Basket*, their once-deluxe burger with cheese and bacon that could now be upgraded to a super-sized meal for an additional 37 cents! A billboard was displayed in the center of town, showing an action shot of Rusty behind the wheel with his logo in bold lively print:

'Go! Rusty, Go!'

Equally important, this surge of popularity had a *trickle-down effect* all of its own.

His elitist dad who was never invited to poker parties couldn't walk near a barber shop or bar without having his past call out to him.

"Hey, Paul, get in here!" would be the cry when spotted.

Dottie was also a *marked woman*.

"Hey, Dottie, we'd better see you at my place tonight for tea!" Such a call, or one in similar fashion, would channel to her in broad daylight.

Unlike before, Paul and his lovely wife developed a liking for walking hand in hand through the middle of town.

Each crew member got hits whenever identified.

Most important, David Smith and his love, Lisa Grimes, were deeply respected in school. This was because David was always pictured in the paper with Golden Hills' Rusty Hampton—and never once bragged about it. *Instead, he treated everyone with the same amount of respect.*

Everything seemed to be in order in Rusty Hampton's life, except for one crucial detail:

The actual contract to be formally offered and signed had not yet been put on the table. Until there was positively a written proposal followed by a signing, Rusty could only feel that he was in a state of limbo.

He constantly reminded himself of Rocco's parting words:

"You'll hear from me once decisions are made."

Words that kept him up at night, wondering if he would actually be chosen.

⁕

Almost two weeks to the day, Rocco Conti had made contact. "I have some good news for you, my friend," he said in a gracious tone.

Arrangements were made to meet with Rocco, his wife, and some of his business associates at the very banquet room they'd met at before. *"And bring everybody!"* he added.

The setting would be like the last one, with one exception. It would be that of a formal occasion where documents were signed, hands were shook, and life got underway.

Chapter XIII

UPON ENTERING THE FAMILIAR BANQUET FACILITY, a noticeable change made its presence known.

The centerpiece ice sculpture was now one of an Indy car with the number *37*. A sure sign that a contract was indeed drawn up. A sigh of relief came over the rising star as the beautiful carving momentarily mesmerized him.

All were present, including the addition of David's mother, aunt, and his future bride. The proud teen who had fate associate him with *the claim to fame of Golden Hills* was beyond grateful. He intensively prayed as he held the Bible his mentor gave him. David would point at it when Rusty saw him. Next he would point to the heavens, and then directly toward Rusty in one motion, all while giving a smile that lit up Rusty's soul.

A tear of approval trickled down Rusty's face as he nodded in agreement. Walking toward the son he chose, Rusty said, "Why don't you wear this for the rest of the evening?"

Out of nowhere came his trademark red hat as he placed it on David's head. Next to the Bible, it was the ultimate compliment he could ever give someone. "You look good in it!" he said in a soft tone. Leaning forward, he whispered into the lad's ear, *"You can give it back to me tomorrow..."*

At that moment Rusty felt a soft kiss on his cheek as his wife walked past to greet friends.

Looking around the room, he was relieved to see that Rocco and his wife were seemingly enjoying a visit with his parents—*and not the Howells.*

Team members were scattered about, making new friends as the buffet table began to tantalize those near and far.

Eventually a certain essence never before felt touched all those who were present.

It was as if the evening was becoming *too perfect...*

ເ★◉໐ເ★◉໐ເ★◉໐

Before the meal, Rocco stood up and gave a toast to Rusty. Everyone joined in with cheers following. It was after the meal when a slightly concerned expression came across Rocco's face. One that prompted him to address his would-be new driver. "Can we talk for a minute?" he asked in a quiet voice.

"Sure," replied an apprehensive Rusty.

Rocco spotted a small circular glass table in the corner. It had bar stools and was tall enough to stand in front of while resting one's hands. Once seated, Rusty fired first. "Is something wrong?" he asked.

"I have one concern," replied the Catholic grandfather. Rusty's eyes met with Rocco's as he continued. "Look," he said. "I admire everything about you as a driver and a person. I even consider your friends and family one with mine." Placing a hand on Rusty's shoulder, he said what he felt he must say. "It's David; *he's simply too young to travel with us.* Besides, he has another path in life to follow..."

It was obvious that Rusty was deeply hurt by the news and took a deep breath. He looked down to digest what he'd just heard. Recovering the best he could, he looked at the compassionate man and began to defend David's value to the team.

Rocco was the one in control and presented a contract that equaled that of his top drivers. "You will probably end up in the Indy Hall Of Fame if you sign with me," he pointed out.

It was the dichotomy of a lifetime—trying to decide between the passion he had throughout his entire life; and a student that he felt compelled to take in and nurture *as a son.*

The boss then applied some pressure. "I have others who would gladly accept any offer from me in a heartbeat. They too are excellent drivers."

It became obvious that there was little time to ponder on this dilemma: Rocco was still on what was to be regarded as a business trip and needed his answer *now.*

Looking away, Rusty saw the boy with the angelical aura watching his hero from across the room. The young man who knew that he would never again be rejected or left behind because of *one Rusty Hampton.*

With his eyes matching that of David's, an astounding discovery was made:

The formally lost soul in the red cap holding the Bible was of the same entity that once ran away from home years ago. The very one who woke up with that very book in his hands. The Good Book he'd read every night that guided him throughout his life.

Rusty realized that whenever he looked at David, it was actually himself as a young boy he saw—*searching for direction.* Immediately, Rocco's words played back in his head: *"Besides, he has another path in life to follow..."*

Rocco was correct.

Without warning, a final spiritual nail was driven into the coffin. Rusty would once again hear the immortal words that never sat well with him: "Remember, Rusty; with me *you'll always have the best money can buy..."*

At that very moment, it became clear to him that it was the Bible that mysteriously entered his life—*and not the expensive go-kart that tricked love out of him*—that was important. Rusty felt an epiphany: he didn't want to race anymore. It was time to follow David and better serve the Lord.

Feeling a tremendous weight lift off his shoulders, Rusty stood up and looked directly at Rocco, stating, "I'm not the right guy for you."

The men shook hands with immense respect and parted ways.

While leaving, the wife with radar walked by and kissed Rusty's cheek while saying:

"And that's why I love you so much..."

Chapter XIV

THE NEXT DAY, RUSTY SUMMONED HIS CREW to inform them of the bad news. The older members immediately figured out *why* the deal fell through.

David, on the other hand, was just young and innocent enough to buy into it and offered encouragement. "There are many out there who know you're the very best!" he said. "You'll be getting more offers in no time."

Rusty thanked David for the emotional support while the older men stared at him in awe. Once the meeting was over, Cliff Wright left last, saying, "I wish I had a dad like you..."

Paul and Dottie were next on the list as their son dropped by.

It was Paul who took it the hardest. Placing a hand on his boy's shoulder, he consoled him. "Look, son," he said in a calm voice. "You probably got caught up in a numbers game. It happens," he said.

"I'm alright, Dad," assured Rusty. The son then attempted to shake his dad's hand while discretely returning the wad of cash he'd recently handed him. Without breaking eye contact, Paul would not clasp Rusty's hand. Instead, he slightly pushed it back while giving a wink at the son he believed in.

It was a week later when Jean visited her in-laws and told them what really took place between Rocco Conti and their son. Paul was overwhelmed beyond words, realizing the sacrifice his son had made.

During their next visit, Paul addressed his son. "Jean told us about the conditions Rocco gave you—and how you stood up to him." Trembling with admiration, he continued, "I'd like to think that I would do something like that."

Rusty smiled at the man who had adopted him and replied, "Where do you think I got it from?"

⚜ ⚜ ⚜

Home life became more livable now that Jean Hampton's marriage had a husband who had more time for her. "You are taking this so well," she commented in a polite tone.

Looking at the woman who'd made his life, he repeated a quote she had delivered many times:

"Haven't you heard? There's more to life that just racing."

Jean enjoyed his comeback and gave a peck on the cheek, followed by a hug that became a lengthy back rub. "Do you still want to race?" she asked.

"Not at this moment," he replied. "I feel so free with the thought of letting go of it."

⚜ ⚜ ⚜

Good news arrived that day; David and Lisa were to graduate soon. They were both invited to the ceremony, along with Paul, Dottie, and the entire crew. "We'll be there!" responded Rusty on the phone. "And congratulations, big guy!"

Paul and Dottie fell in love with David and Lisa long ago. They were honored to attend the graduation ceremony and insisted that everyone come to their home for a dinner party afterwards. It was there when the young couple made a formal announcement. They were to get married and pursue their calling in ministry.

There was more. It was Rusty himself who David picked to be his best man. In Rusty's book, *that was an honor that greatly surpassed any race.*

How right he was.

Eventually the newlyweds were living in a rental house a few doors down from where his mother and aunt lived. David and Lisa were also holding two jobs while attending classes. David worked at a local car lot cleaning cars, doing odd jobs, and assisting customers. Lisa was the traditional waitress in a local cafe. Together, they worked part-time at their church and volunteered massive hours: *a labor of love that they would not have any other way.*

Bible studies became common at David and Lisa's place, with a motivated Rusty Hampton attending. The very Bible he gave to his subject was now the focal point in comforting others. *In fact, it inspired him along with his wife and parents to get baptized.*

On occasion, David and Lisa would each deliver a heartfelt sermon in church that would penetrate one's soul, messages that further guided one down the Lord's path. In time, their first child was on the way. The ultimate gift for a boy from a broken home. Again, it was Rusty who was chosen to be the godfather.

David Smith and his wife, Lisa, had their life secured by following the right path. Soon they would be called on for their spiritual strength:

Rusty Hampton was about to face his greatest fear.

Chapter XV

RUSTY HAMPTON BEGAN TO SEARCH for mundane jobs that weren't associated with the racing world. A simpler life that would include more time for his better half and more time for family. It would also allow his life to get more involved in the faith that beckoned to him.

It wasn't such a hard decision to leave the racing world. He gave it his very best and covered more ground than the other ninety-nine percent who tried. He took the time to explain this decision at his final crew meeting.

"It was a good run," commented Roger Blackstone.

"Just remember," said Rusty. "We're all family for life. If I ever go a few weeks not hearing from one of you, that will be *me* pounding on your front door!"

It was official: Team Hampton had dissolved.

⟡⟡⟡⟡⟡

The civilian life for one Stanley Victor 'Rusty' Hampton was a forgiving one. It even seemed to give back a few years that his former fast-paced life had taxed from him. The color on his face and lightness in his walk served as testimony.

In time, fewer and fewer stopped to talk to the local celebrity. By his own free will, that chapter in his life was now in the past. What he really wanted was to finish out his life as a simple, non-complicated common man. One who drew no attention at all. He also wanted to be more active in his local church, like David and Lisa.

Rusty now looked forward to coming home and helping his wife cook dinner. A walk would usually ensue later, with the possibility of a dessert thrown in somewhere.

Rusty was at peace. It would be fair to say that his marriage was comparable to that of the Smiths:

They were far from being rich and only wanted to be together—working together! A priceless combination...

One evening in front of the fireplace, Jean initiated a conversation. "You have done everything that I have always felt was in you."

The man holding her digested what was said and pondered on it. *"What do you mean by that?"* he asked.

Kissing him, she continued. "You have done it all," she said. "You did racing on your terms and even got the highest offer a driver could get. You became the greatest son your parents could ever have, which has made their lives happy beyond words." There was more. "You also gave David a reason to live and to be somebody. *You* are the reason why he found the Lord and is happily married."

Rusty started to get scared and asked, "Is there something wrong?"

"No," she replied. "I loved you from the moment I first saw you on the playground. I knew that you were dealt an unfair hand in life, and that you *were very special.* Everything that tried to stop you, couldn't. Instead, you never quit and made lives better—like mine."

"What are you trying to say?" he asked.

"My battle with cancer has advanced to a terminal state," she calmly said. "It's nobody's fault," she added. "It's probably because you've arrived as you were meant to—and that I am no longer needed."

Rusty was never told of her cancer and tensed up.

"NO!" he cried out. "I finally realized that all that other stuff was meaningless! This is the first time in my life that I've found happiness; I only have to be with you!"

The strong woman laughed and had a response. "I'm not going anywhere," she said. "I'll probably be the reason why you mysteriously find your keys and discover an old bill in one of your pockets."

The child who always existed held onto the love of his life and emotionally fell apart. Patting her man on the back, she reminded him in a comforting tone, "Don't worry. I'll still be here for a while..."

Hours passed in silence, and then the phone rang.

It took all of Rusty's strength to get up and answer it. His father was on the other end. "Son, I don't know how to tell you this, but your mother isn't doing well..."

❦ ❦ ❦ ❦

Rusty sat with his father at the dinner table he grew up with. Within moments, he learned of his mother having been diagnosed with Alzheimer's disease some time ago.

"She was so happy and proud of you, son," explained the father. "The physicians stressed that we take one day at a time with her and make no sudden changes." Looking at his son, he pointed out, "You couldn't have been any closer to her. For that reason, I held back saying anything, since it is a condition we cannot change." Looking down, he continued. "Your mother has deteriorated to the point where she's showing dementia. They told me that she doesn't have much time left."

Rusty looked down in tears grasping the situation. Looking up to his teary-eyed father, he mustered up all of his strength. It was now his turn to share the same parity *his* wife was going through.

Placing a hand on his son's shoulder, the father said in a somber tone:

"We men need to stick together..."

Chapter XVI

THE FATHER-AND-SON DUO of Paul and Rusty Hampton could be viewed as an updated Team Hampton. *A different kind of winning team.*

Together, they attended counseling through both physicians and David's church. In time, both came to terms with the situation—and accepted it. Knowing that their faith would be tested, they remained diligent and catered to their wives the best they could.

"It's always in the Lord's hands," David would point out. He then elaborated further:

"Never lose sight that all of us are walking through life. Eventually, we reunite with one another when we come home to Him."

Paul and Rusty knew that David was right. From there, they lived knowing that in time they would be reunited with their wives *forever.*

In their own way, they continued the *Hampton Racing legacy* by serving the town they lived in. Namely, by offering their services to the church that David and Lisa belonged to, and eventually becoming deacons.

One day a message delivered from David made their world stand still. The Hampton men had a free day and offered their services to the church. David scratched his head, trying to find a loose end that needed to be tied. At once an idea popped into his head, making him call out,

"Hey, there is one thing that I keep forgetting to do…" He then spoke of how it was agreed that a small coffee table would fit perfectly in the church's lobby. "It would the first thing a newcomer would see when they entered our church," he explained. "We would always have plenty of Bibles on it, free for the taking. It will be a way to introduce the Lord to anyone in need of guidance."

Paul and Rusty certainly knew what happens when a Bible is gifted to someone in need—and could only wholeheartedly agree with the brilliant idea. "Rusty and I will go out and find a good one at a furniture store," said Paul.

David then had his spiritual mode kick into high gear as heavenly words flowed gracefully through his heart. "Don't worry," he said.

"It doesn't have to be the best money can buy…"

That comment registered deep and gave a *jolt* to both men. Without any thought, each slowly turned to the other, knowing where that message *actually came from*. More importantly, *they both understood who it was meant for.*

⊙⋙⊙⋘⊙⋙⊙⋘⊙⋙⊙

Soon a baby shower for Lisa had the women of the entire congregation join *with Jean and Dottie present*. It was a traditional welcoming wagon for a young man who would be named *David Rusty Smith*.

Throughout the upcoming year, the families would rotate on whose household would hold the next Bible study or barbeque, all while getting further spiritually connected and watching little David grow.

Equally important, the men were getting to know each other on a different playing field. Boldly, they compared childhood escapades and dreams that had faded long ago. Stories with admissions of guilt attached *that were never to be repeated.*

One day in church, Paul elbowed Rusty and pointed at the altar. On the corner was the Bible that Rusty had given the future pastor long ago. "I remember placing that very book in your hands as a child," he whispered. "You were so cute with that red hat on. I thought that I'd throw a blanket over you once you fell asleep and pass on the Good Book that my father had given me when I was that age."

Rusty slowly turned his head and looked at his father with astonishment. The puzzle that had eluded him for years was finally solved, and it came from who could only be considered as his best friend!"

A special bond was deepened that implied brotherhood.

❧ ⚜ ❧ ⚜ ❧ ⚜

It was little David's second birthday, with a fading Dottie and Jean still present. It was amazing that the husbands who prayed together could still relish those special lives, *for whatever reason...*

The focus was now on the toddler who was fascinated with his new toys and the boxes they came in. Stumbling about, he noticed a plastic replica of a racing car and motioned toward it. Immediately, Rusty called out from the peanut gallery. Projecting a voice just loud enough for his father to hear, he cried out:

"Bad race car, bad!" Using his hands to channel the sides of his mouth, he continued. "Get away from that! You won't have any money!"

The rugrat who was too distant to hear the warning shot hobbled over to a plastic desk with a make-believe computer and matching cell phone. It was now Paul's turn.

"Gadzooks! Get away from those things; *you won't have any friends!"*

The child continued to move about aimlessly as he inspected his goldmine. In time, both men were relieved to see the infant come across a bright red plastic fireman's hat and place it on his head.

Rusty looked around and saw the comfortable lounge chair where his mother sat. Commenting to his future roommate, he said, "Mom seems happy..."

"She is," replied Paul.

Jean came out of nowhere and kissed Rusty on the cheek. Spreading her arms, the thin, feeble woman said, "All of this because of you."

54

Rusty surveyed the sight with great satisfaction as he watched David and Lisa share their family. The teenage couple that realized they were meant to have a life together *regardless of their critics.* "Every battle you fought set the stage for this family to exist," she added.

Pointing at the two-year-old, she drove in the final stake that stood as a victory for all. "That boy got to enter this life the normal way, because of what a famous race car driver did for his father years ago."

That comment sent Rusty back through time. He recalled the many underdogs he had befriended in life and stood up for. Outcasts who were merely good souls marching to a different beat. He also remembered the morning when he was a scared boy who woke up holding a Bible—The very book that encouraged him every night to march forward.

It suddenly occurred to him that he never actually wanted to be deemed a conqueror or champion. He just wanted all to know that he was there whenever an injustice had to be dealt with. *A servant of our Lord.* Equally important, he fully understood that everyone present, including himself, would eventually enter God's Kingdom— where Jean and Dottie would be waiting. *The real path in life that money could never buy.*

It became a moment where one Stanley Victor *Rusty* Hampton felt all of his problems leave his body. He was now existing in a world that only allowed him to feel good about himself. *It could never be contested that he always had the Lord's blessing as he trudged through life.*

Giving her patented kiss on the cheek, she finished by saying:

"And that's why I love you so much..."

The End

Epilogue

STANLEY VICTOR 'RUSTY' HAMPTON began life looking for his identity, and more important- a home.

In the beginning the bewildered youth lived an existence of being tossed around like a hot potato. A defeating cycle that circled around detention centers and failed foster homes. Along this path he learned to have empathy for others and to defend justice. A quality that could only stem from his past, and identifying others who were also dealt a cruel hand.

One fateful day Rusty hit the jackpot. An elder couple from the upper crust chose him specifically to be their only child. The adopted youth was now in a lavish environment *where money was no object.* From there a fork in the river presented itself: On one hand he was mysteriously gifted a Bible. On the other, love was tricked out of him when he received a motorized racing toy that would be the envy of any kid.

It was only natural for the gold standard of any Boy to present itself. Despite the subtle impact that the Good Book was already making; it still took a back seat to the high-powered racing machine. That was until Rusty met his past through a fourteen- year- old boy, *who too was lost.*

A calling was now set in motion.

Rusty Hampton's sparkling race car and successful career was what drew young David Smith's attention. Knowing this, Rusty righted what was wrongged by accepting him. The local racer then set him on the 'right track' by gifting him the very Bible that entered his life long ago. The spiritual source that saturated him with love and encouragement.

A poetic justice was now in the making.

Rusty was indeed the voice of experience and knew how to handle the impressionable teen who was now idolizing him. His new friend now possessed the very Bible that always guided him through his darkest moments. The Good Book that had tailor-made messages *for everyone.*

What happened next spread like wildfire. It would soon be that very book having David leading others to the kingdom of our Lord!

It all started when a lost soul was gifted a Bible; and then passed it on to another lost soul.

The ultimate gift.

Matt Shea

About Matt Shea

MATT SHEA IS A DEVELOPING AUTHOR having published eight paperbacks and twelve e-books. He is greatly inspired by the writings of Andy Griffith and focuses on the common folk that small towns are made of.

He credits the success of his first book, 'The Groundskeeper And Other Short Stories' to his family. The values that were instilled throughout his childhood gave him the strong sense of justice that is conveyed through his writings. The Shea family is only an average American family from an average neighborhood. Their secret was that they were close knit and accepted others.

Matt's mother, Vyerl set an example of being self sacrificing; having never placed herself first. She always cared about the feelings of others, no matter who they were. She even sponsored many foster children despite having a family of eight. During the holidays, the Roman Catholic mom would also have a Hanukkah bush for their Jewish friends. There were years when the family would make Christmas gifts and personally deliver them to seniors in rest homes.

The very table that Matt initially wrote all of his stories on came from a childhood neighbor, Netta Wilson. Through time, Netta had to be relocated to assistant living due to deteriorating health. Vyerl never forgot that she and Netta traveled to see the Vatican together. Care packages, visits, and transporting Netta to spend Sundays at their home became a ritual until her last day. When she passed away, Matt was bequeathed an antique table from Netta. A priceless heirloom that he regards as sacred.

Many of Matt's friends are senior citizens or foreign born. He has the common practice of brewing a pot of tea and inviting them over to watch Alfred Hitchcock. Together they will watch Alfred, share a cup of tea, and afterwords listen to his manuscripts. Sometimes these social gatherings last well beyond midnight. "This is where I get most of my ideas," says Matt. "I learned this from my mom."

Matt Shea appreciates all who take the time to read his stories. He loves feedback and offers his email address for any comments or suggestions you might have. Matt promises to do his very best to answer all who write him. His goal is to reach out to his audience and improve as a writer and a person.

worknmatt7@aol.com
www.mattsheabooks.com

Laura Shea with her dad, author Matt Shea.

Books by Matt Shea

More Uplifting
Stories From
Matt Shea Books!

Matt Shea

www.ingramcontent.com/pod-product-compliance
Lightning Source LLC
Chambersburg PA
CBHW071346130626
46556CB00005B/2053